# MR. FUNNY

by Roger Hargreaves

Mr Funny lived in a teapot!

It had two bedrooms, a bathroom, a kitchen and a living room, and it suited Mr Funny very nicely.

One day, Mr Funny was having lunch.

He wasn't very hungry, so he only had a daisy sandwich and a glass of toast!

"Delicious," he murmured to himself as he finished his funny lunch.

After lunch Mr Funny decided to go for a drive in his car.

Mr Funny's car was a shoe!

Have you ever seen a car that looks like a shoe?

It looks very funny!

As he drove along, everybody who saw him laughed to see such a funny sight.

He passed a worm at the side of the road.

The worm thought Mr Funny in his funny car was the funniest thing he had ever seen.

He nearly laughed himself in two!

He passed a pig in a field.

The pig thought Mr Funny in his funny car was the funniest thing that she had ever seen.

She nearly laughed her tail off!

Even the flowers he passed thought that Mr Funny was the funniest thing that they had ever seen.

They nearly laughed themselves out of the ground!

Eventually Mr Funny came to some crossroads.

He didn't know which way to go, so he looked at the signpost.

One of the signs said TO THE ZOO.

"That will be fun," thought Mr Funny to himself, so he drove his shoe towards the zoo.

When he arrived at the gate of the zoo, he stopped.

It was closed.

"I'm sorry," said the zoo keeper. "We've had to close the zoo because all the animals have colds, and they're all feeling very sorry for themselves."

"Oh dear," said Mr Funny, and then he thought. "Perhaps I can help to cheer them up," he said.

"Well," said the zoo keeper, "it's worth a try." And he opened the gate.

Mr Funny drove into the zoo.

In his shoe.

The first thing he saw was an elephant. It was true. The elephant was feeling very sorry for herself. Very sorry indeed.

Mr Funny stood and looked at the sad-looking elephant.

And the sad-looking elephant stood and looked at Mr Funny.

Oh dear!

Then, do you know what Mr Funny did?

He pulled a funny face!

Mr Funny, as you'd imagine, is very good at pulling funny faces.

The elephant giggled.

She'd never seen anything so funny.

Mr Funny pulled another funny face.

The elephant burst out laughing.

The elephant laughed and laughed and laughed.

She laughed so hard, she nearly laughed her trunk off!

And she felt a lot lot better.

Mr Funny went over to the lion house.

There was a lion, feeling extraordinarily sorry for himself.

Mr Funny stood and looked at the sad-looking lion.

And the sad-looking lion stood and looked at Mr Funny.

Oh dear!

And then Mr Funny pulled the funniest looking face that's probably ever been pulled anywhere, ever.

Now, you've heard a lion roar before, haven't you?

Well this lion roared too – with laughter.

He laughed so hard he nearly laughed his whiskers to pieces.

Then Mr Funny went around to see all the other animals in the zoo.

Oh dear, what a miserable-looking lot!

For all of them, Mr Funny pulled funnier and funnier faces.

The big brown bear giggled, and then burst out laughing.

And the giraffe laughed so hard she nearly laughed her neck into a knot. And the hippopotamus nearly laughed himself out of his skin. And the penguins nearly laughed their flippers floppy. And the leopard, well, you really should have seen him, he laughed so hard he nearly laughed his spots off!

What a pandemonium!

"Oh Mr Funny," giggled the zoo keeper, who had started laughing as well. "Oh Mr Funny, thank you very very much indeed for coming to cheer us all up!"

"Oh, it was nothing really," replied Mr Funny modestly, and drove off.

In his shoe!

Later, when Mr Funny arrived home, he chuckled to himself. "Well," he said. "That's the end of another funny day!"

And he parked his shoe and went inside his teapot and, because he was feeling thirsty, he made himself . . .

. . . a nice hot cup of cake!

# **3** Great Offers for MR.MEN Fans!

## **1** New Mr. Men or Little Miss Library Bus Presentation Cases

A brand new stronger, roomier school bus library box, with sturdy carrying handle and stay-closed fasteners.
The full colour, wipe-clean boxes make a great home for your full collection.
They're just £5.99 inc P&P and free bookmark!

☐ MR. MEN  ☐ LITTLE MISS (please tick and order overleaf)

## **2** Door Hangers and Posters

PLEASE STICK YOUR 50P COIN HERE

In every Mr. Men and Little Miss book like this one, you will find a special token. Collect 6 tokens and we will send you a brilliant Mr. Men or Little Miss poster and a Mr. Men or Little Miss double sided full colour bedroom door hanger of your choice. Simply tick your choice in the list and tape a 50p coin for your two items to this page.

**Door Hangers** (please tick)
☐ Mr. Nosey & Mr. Muddle
☐ Mr. Slow & Mr. Busy
☐ Mr. Messy & Mr. Quiet
☐ Mr. Perfect & Mr. Forgetful
☐ Little Miss Fun & Little Miss Late
☐ Little Miss Helpful & Little Miss Tidy
☐ Little Miss Busy & Little Miss Brainy
☐ Little Miss Star & Little Miss Fun

**Posters** (please tick)
☐ MR.MEN
☐ LITTLE MISS

CUT ALONG DOTTED LINE AND RETURN THIS WHOLE PAGE

## 3 Sixteen Beautiful Fridge Magnets – any **2** for £2.00! inc P&P

They're very special collector's items!
Simply tick your first and second* choices from the list below
of any 2 characters!

### 1st Choice

- [ ] Mr. Happy
- [ ] Mr. Lazy
- [ ] Mr. Topsy-Turvy
- [ ] Mr. Bounce
- [ ] Mr. Bump
- [ ] Mr. Small
- [ ] Mr. Snow
- [ ] Mr. Wrong
- [ ] Mr. Daydream
- [ ] Mr. Tickle
- [ ] Mr. Greedy
- [ ] Mr. Funny
- [ ] Little Miss Giggles
- [ ] Little Miss Splendid
- [ ] Little Miss Naughty
- [ ] Little Miss Sunshine

### 2nd Choice

- [ ] Mr. Happy
- [ ] Mr. Lazy
- [ ] Mr. Topsy-Turvy
- [ ] Mr. Bounce
- [ ] Mr. Bump
- [ ] Mr. Small
- [ ] Mr. Snow
- [ ] Mr. Wrong
- [ ] Mr. Daydream
- [ ] Mr. Tickle
- [ ] Mr. Greedy
- [ ] Mr. Funny
- [ ] Little Miss Giggles
- [ ] Little Miss Splendid
- [ ] Little Miss Naughty
- [ ] Little Miss Sunshine

*Only in case your first choice is out of stock.

--- **TO BE COMPLETED BY AN ADULT** ---

To apply for any of these great offers, ask an adult to complete the coupon below and send it with
the appropriate payment and tokens, if needed, to MR. MEN OFFERS, PO BOX 7, MANCHESTER M19 2HD

- [ ] Please send _____ Mr. Men Library case(s) and/or _____ Little Miss Library case(s) at £5.99 each inc P&P
- [ ] Please send a poster and door hanger as selected overleaf. I enclose six tokens plus a 50p coin for P&P
- [ ] Please send me _____ pair(s) of Mr. Men/Little Miss fridge magnets, as selected above at £2.00 inc P&P

**Fan's Name** _____

**Address** _____

_____ **Postcode** _____

**Date of Birth** _____

**Name of Parent/Guardian** _____

**Total amount enclosed £** _____

- [ ] **I enclose a cheque/postal order payable to Egmont Books Limited**
- [ ] **Please charge my MasterCard/Visa/Amex/Switch or Delta account** (delete as appropriate)

| | | | | | | | | | | | | | | | |
|---|---|---|---|---|---|---|---|---|---|---|---|---|---|---|---|

Card Number

**Expiry date** ___/___ **Signature** _____

**MR.MEN   LITTLE MISS**
Mr. Men and Little Miss™ & ©Mrs. Roger Hargreaves

CUT ALONG DOTTED LINE AND RETURN THIS WHOLE PAGE